# My Zombie Valentine

# My Zombie Valentine

## DIAN CURTIS REGAN

AN
**APPLE**
PAPERBACK

SCHOLASTIC INC.
New York Toronto London Auckland Sydney

ISBN 0-590-46038-2

12 11 10 9 8 7 6 5 4 3 2 1            3 4 5 6 7 8/9

Printed in the U.S.A.            28

First Scholastic printing, January 1993

*For Edward Bryant,*
*who respects zombies for who they are*

# Contents

# Contents

# My Zombie Valentine

# 1.
# The New Girl

**I**t was love at first fright.

Joey Ocean was doing his *gozintos*, which is what he and his friends called long division. (As in: three *gozinto* twenty-four eight times.)

With a sudden *whoosh* of wind, the door to Mr. Bramble's sixth-grade class blew open. A curious hush settled over the entire math class.

Joey watched papers on the bulletin board flutter in the breeze. A foreboding sense of eeriness tap-danced inside his chest the same way it had last Saturday at the theater when the opening shot of *Attack of the Toxic Teachers* flashed onto the screen.

Mr. Bramble rose from his desk as the sound of slow footsteps shuffled in the hallway.

Then *she* walked into the room.

And into Joey Ocean's life.

She was tall. Maybe that's why she caught his eye at first. He was the tallest guy in the sixth grade. He'd been the tallest guy in *every* grade since kindergarten.

Sometimes it was embarrassing. Like at class picture time when the photographer asked if he was standing on a box in the back row.

Or when Mr. Bramble stood next to him, and Joey had to bend his knees to look the teacher straight in the eyes.

Or when he got paired off to square dance with someone like Mashika Chan, who barely came up to his elbow.

But the new girl — the girl who made the hair on the back of his neck stand on end — *she* towered over Mr. Bramble, too. Just like Joey. It was the first thing he noticed about her.

The second thing he noticed was her hair.

Her hair was the color of October.

And just as windblown.

Joey glanced at the row of windows to see if one was open, blowing gusts of February's frigid chill into the room, swirling the girl's radiant hair about her thin shoulders.

The windows were closed.

His mind struggled for a word to pinpoint the exact shade of her locks. Their brilliant hue fell somewhere between the color of a ripe pumpkin, a russet leaf, and a polished apple.

Vinnie Capaldi reached across the aisle and punched Joey's shoulder. "Who is *that?*" he asked in a loud whisper.

2

"Class," Mr. Bramble said, as if answering Vinnie's question. "Please welcome our new student."

The teacher studied a piece of paper the girl handed him. "Her name is Xia Dedd," he added, writing it on the board with brisk strokes of the chalk:

*XIA*

Under that he wrote: ZEE YAH, then tossed the chalk into the air and caught it. *"Zee yah,"* Mr. Bramble said, putting his teeth together to drag out the vowels. "Say it with me, class, ZEEEEE YAAAAH."

The class moaned the name in unison. Joey thought it sounded like the wail of a dying walrus.

Beside him, Vinnie shook in silent laughter. His head bobbed up and down in rhythm with his pudgy stomach as he scribbled a note, then passed it to Joey:

*So why didn't her parents make it easy on all of us and spell her name Zeeeee Yaaaaah?*

An unexpected urge to defend the girl's honor swirled anger through Joey's chest. The impulse startled and scared him at the same time. He whipped sideways and glared at Vinnie. "There's

3

nothing *wrong* with the way her name is spelled. I think it's cool."

Vinnie reared back in his desk, making the front legs come off the floor. "Excuse me, Ocean, but I don't like people with weird names. Xia is a weird name."

"So is Capaldi."

Vinnie punched him in the shoulder again before he could block it.

Joey rubbed his shoulder. Why was he protecting a total stranger? All he knew about the girl was her name.

Mr. Bramble was reading the rest of the note about Xia, telling the class where she came from, but Joey missed it because of Vinnie. He wanted to raise his hand and ask the teacher to tell the story again, but he knew he'd be groaned out of the classroom in disgrace.

The teacher assigned Xia an empty desk in the second row.

Joey's heart ached. Why couldn't she have the empty desk next to his?

"Hey," Mashika Chan said in a grumbly voice. "I can't see around her big hair."

"*Me, neither,*" echoed the rest of the row.

Mr. Bramble squinted across the room, fumbling through papers on the desk for his glasses. He shoved them on and peered down the rows. "Xia, why don't you move to the back, since you're, uh, so tall."

4

Joey watched Xia collect her things. As she rose, his heart rose with her. His eyes followed her across the front of the room and down the aisle.

*His* aisle.

She walked slowly, her movements stiff and jerky. She moved the same way he did on nights after he'd fallen off his skateboard fifty times.

"Oh, man," Vinnie groaned. "Bram's putting her back here with us."

Sometimes Vinnie acted as if he owned the back of the room, like it was his personal territory.

As the new girl drew closer, the breeze that seemed to surround her reached Joey, riffling his hair. The gusty air was cool — not icy cold, yet not as warm as the air in the room.

Watching her walk toward him thrilled him and chilled him at the same time. A sense of foreboding still bubbled inside his chest.

Absently, he smoothed his dark hair with one hand, unable to keep his gaze from following her awkward movements.

The girl glanced his way before sitting down. Joey caught his breath.

Her eyes were the color of mint ice cream.

And just as cold.

Her look alone was enough to freeze him through his heaviest sweater, as though a glacier moved down the aisle instead of a person.

But he smiled anyway.

5

Xia seemed startled by his quick grin. She watched him with guarded suspicion as she took her seat and slid her things into the desk.

Joey's mouth fell open in amazement. Her knees hit the underside of the desk! Just like his! Already they had so much in common.

He wondered who was taller. Him? Or — gasp — her? Was it possible?

He couldn't wait until recess to find out.

# 2.
# You Are in
# My Power

"**W**ake up, Ocean."

"Huh?"

"What's *with* you?" Vinnie's face was inches from Joey's. "The bell rang. Let's go or teams'll already be chosen."

Joey shook his head to clear the fog, then glanced around the empty room. He had no recollection of the last fifteen minutes — the time between the arrival of the new girl and the recess bell.

"O-cean!" Vinnie snarled from the door.

Joey jerked to attention, rushing to follow his impatient friend. What had happened? How could his brain have gone on vacation without him?

A cold blast of winter air slapped his face as he followed Vinnie outside. It reminded him that he'd left his jacket on its hook in the classroom.

"Be right back," he hollered.

"Oh, man!" Vinnie grimaced at him, then raced across the blacktop.

Joey ventured down the hall to Mr. Bramble's room on tiptoe. Kids weren't allowed in the building during recess, coat or no coat.

Making it to the room without being seen, he dashed to the back and grabbed his jacket. Whirling past his desk, he tossed off the pencil he'd been clutching in his hand ever since his heart had been turned upside down.

His world seemed different now. He barely remembered the old Joey Ocean, doing his *gozintos*. That must have happened in another lifetime. On another planet. In another galaxy.

As he started to leave, his gaze fell upon Xia's desk. Joey paused. There it was — her desk, her chair, her notebook paper sticking out one corner with something scribbled on it.

Wait a minute. Joey moved closer. The word "Ocean" jumped off the page and stabbed him in the eyeball. Had Mr. Bramble been discussing *oceans* before recess? In math class?

*Right, Joey,* came Vinnie's voice inside his head. *As in "How many glasses of water would it take to fill the Atlantic Ocean?"*

Joey glanced around. No one was there. Of course no one was there, he told himself, or he'd be thrown outside faster than his little sister Lacy could answer a ringing telephone.

Joey took hold of Xia's paper, tugging it into view so he could read what she'd written. What she'd written was his name — his *full* name, middle name and all: Joseph Milford Ocean.

He let go of the paper as if it were made of nuclear waste. "Holy jets," he whispered. How did *she* know his name? Did Mr. Bramble introduce the entire class to her while Joey's brain was out to lunch?

Impossible. First of all, his name was the only one on the paper, and second, no one knew his middle name — not even Vinnie. Joey would space walk without a lifeline before he'd tell anyone his middle name.

Most kids were named after someone important, like one of their grandparents. Joey was named after his grandparents' *dog*.

Milford. A dirty-white, shag-haired mutt with clumpy fur. A beloved member of the Ocean family for nineteen years.

Milford died the night Joey was born. In their sorrow, the family voted to pay tribute to the loyal pet by bestowing his name on the newest Ocean. Joey knew it was no coincidence that the memorable day he came into the world and ol' Milford departed was a Friday the 13th.

Even though the family was mushy and sentimental about Milford, Joey didn't share their mush. He wasn't honored, only humiliated.

He'd tried. He'd even studied piles of family photos — always blurred because the hyper dog wouldn't stand still. But Joey never mustered any kind of emotional connection with his namesake.

Especially since Lacy thought the whole thing was so incredibly hilarious. She was born three years after him, solely for the purpose of reminding the world that her brother was named for a bumbling dog.

When Grandpa Ocean told Lacy the whole boring story one boring Thanksgiving Day, he spiced up his boring tale by adding: *"Maybe after Milford died, he came back to life again as a person."* Meaning: *"Your brother was a dog in a previous life, Lacy, so why don't you treat him like one in this life?"*

"I hope you have a good explanation for being inside during recess."

Mr. Bramble's voice snapped Joey back to the classroom. "Um, well, I forgot my jacket, so . . ." He held it out as proof he wasn't lying.

Mr. Bramble moved closer, taking a sip from a coffee mug which read: *Fortysomething and still in the sixth grade.* "I don't believe that's *your* desk you're rummaging through, is it?"

Joey bent his knees and rolled his shoulders forward, trying to shrink a couple of inches. A teacher might not like being shorter than an eleven-year-old. "I — I'm not rummaging. I was returning a pencil to — "

"Well, you should have waited until after recess." Mr. Bramble glanced at the clock, waving Joey away. "Go on, get outside."

With pleasure, Joey thought, scrambling for the door.

The soccer game was at its noisy mid-point, as he knew it would be. No point trying to get on the field now. He wandered across the blacktop, glad not to be involved in a game after all. What he really wanted to do was look for Xia Dedd.

She was easy to spot, a full head taller than the other girls. She wore no coat, but didn't look the least bit cold, even though the wind-chill factor must have been near zero.

Surrounding her was "the group," led by Suzanne Varney and Mashika Chan. Joey should have known they'd be the first to check out the new girl, then decide on the spot if she was okay, weird, geeky, or a threat — meaning smarter or prettier than they were.

The girls had Xia backed against the brick wall of the school. She seemed spooked, like a fox caught in a trap, frantically searching for a way to escape.

Joey drew close to hear their conversation.

"Well, fine," Mashika was saying, "if that's the way you want to be." She whipped around, her dark straight hair flopping about the padded shoulders on her jacket.

The group didn't whip around with her, which obviously annoyed Mashika because she liked to be the boss. "Come on, guys," she said in a huff.

"The new girl is too good to talk to us."

Stepping away in unison, they kept their eyes glued to Xia, as if afraid to turn their backs for fear she'd do something weird — like zap them with a hidden raygun.

"No." Joey blocked their departure.

"No, *what*?" Mashika asked, giving him her deluxe sneer.

"She doesn't think she's too good to talk to you." Joey motioned at Xia. "She's just, well, she's shy, and she doesn't like to talk."

"How do *you* know?"

Joey was wondering the same thing. How did *he* know what Xia was thinking? With intense curiosity, he studied her face, as though her freckles had suddenly lined up in letters, creating a secret message across her cheeks that only he could read.

The group parted, bringing him face-to-face with the girl who was. . . . Yes! She was the same height as he was! Not taller. Not shorter. The exact same height.

Joey gazed into her mint ice cream eyes. And he knew.

He knew what she was thinking.

He didn't know *how* he knew, but what she was thinking was: *Thank you for speaking for me.*

*You're welcome*, Joey answered without saying a word.

# 3.
# The Girl of His Dreams

"**H**ey, Fido, dinner's ready."

Joey glanced up from the pile of reference books scattered around him on the floor in his room. Lacy's grin looked sinister these days, with two front teeth missing.

"The name's *Joey*," he said in a bored voice. How could a third-grader be such a smart aleck? He wasn't like that when *he* was in the third grade. At least he hoped not.

Turning his attention back to the book in his lap, Joey scanned the article about mental telepathy. How was it possible for one person to know what another was thinking?

The book hadn't told him any more than he already knew. Joey sighed. What had he expected to find in the encyclopedia? A picture of Xia next to an article about strange powers?

Strange powers. The words gave Joey his quota of goose bumps for the rest of the decade.

Sitting here safely at home, the idea of mind-talking terrified him. Yet while it was happening, he'd accepted it, welcomed it. Why? How had she done it? And why had she chosen Joseph Milford Ocean as the privileged one? The one to receive her messages?

Joey had to admit, he was flattered. Did Xia like him? As much as he liked her? Did she notice how tall he was? She had to look *down* at everyone else, but *him* she could see eye-to-eye.

"Jo-ey!"

"Coming, Mom!" He slammed the encyclopedias shut and shoved them back onto the shelf. His long legs took the stairs three at a time as he headed toward the kitchen.

Mrs. Ocean was still dressed in her snazzy exercise clothes from teaching the Junior Jazzercise class. Her dark hair was caught up in a curly pony tail. She did three *pliés* as she chopped the lettuce.

Lacy imitated her mom. Set a plate on the table. *Plié*. Set a glass on the table. *Plié*. She, too, was dressed in the green leotard and plaid tights she'd worn to Mom's class, her own curly hair in a pony tail.

Joey thought she looked like a miniature version of Mom — only Mom had front teeth.

"Anything interesting happen at school today?" his mother asked, scooping a turkey burger onto Joey's plate in the middle of a side stretch.

He paused to shake a bottle of ketchup before opening it. What should he say? Sure, Mom, the

14

most wonderful thing in the world happened. I fell in love. With a tall redhead who can read my mind.

"Naw," he answered, scooping sprout and tofu salad onto his plate. "Nothing happened."

But his own thoughts stopped him. Could Xia *really* read his mind? The way he'd read hers? Or was her power even greater? How deep inside him could she see? If she knew what he was *saying* mentally, did she also know what he was thinking? Feeling? The color of his underwear?

Holy jets, Joey exclaimed to himself, I'd better be careful what I think. This could get really embarrassing.

"That's not what *I* heard," Lacy said. A pickle slice disappeared through the gap in her front teeth. "I heard your class got a new girl who's weird, weird, *weird*! Suzanne said she acts like a zombie."

"A what?" Mom asked as Joey's brain echoed the question.

"A zombie." Lacy stuck both arms out straight and fixed a blank stare on the refrigerator magnets. "I *vant* to *suck* your *blu-ud*," she singsonged.

Joey laughed, but Lacy's words chased an uneasy tingle up his spine. "Zombies don't suck blood," he explained. "Vampires do. You've got your monsters mixed up."

"Excuse me?" Mom waved a spatula at Lacy.

15

"What are you talking about? How do you know what goes on in Joey's class?"

"They spy on us," Joey answered. "Life in the third grade is so boring, they send spies to find out what *we're* doing."

Lacy wrinkled her lip at him.

"Well, it's true." He sipped his Gatorade. "We don't spy on the *seventh* grade to see what's going on in *their* classroom."

"You can't. They're not in our building." Lacy lowered her voice as if hidden microphones might pick up what she was about to say. "You guys don't have to spy on anyone. You've got plenty of excitement right there in Mr. Bramble's room."

She shot him a jack-o-lantern grin. "Just imagine. A real-live zombie! Or should I say, a real-*dead* zombie?" She cackled like a witch on late-night cable.

Suddenly losing his appetite, Joey shoved away his plate.

Was it true? Could his little sister be right for once?

Was the girl of his dreams really . . . *dead?*

# 4.
# Mind Over Matter

*A mind, stretched to a new idea, never
goes back to its original dimension.*
— OLIVER WENDELL HOLMES

Joey copied the quote from the board. Normally, Mr. Bramble's daily "pearls of wisdom" garnered nothing more than a quick glance, but today, Oliver Wendell Holmes's words jumped off the board and landed in Joey's lap.

Isn't that how he'd felt yesterday? That he was different now? His mind knew something it hadn't known before, and it could never go back to the way it used to be.

"As you know, class," Mr. Bramble was saying. "We will celebrate Valentine's Day on Friday, because the 14th falls on Saturday this year."

"All ri-ight!" Vinnie exclaimed, along with the rest of the class. Joey knew the cheers were not so much for the holiday itself, but in anticipation

17

of a math-and-science-free afternoon.

And he knew what else it meant. It meant Friday was none other than Friday the 13th. The same unlucky day that he was born and Milford died — twelve whole years ago.

Well, he wouldn't think about it. He'd concentrate on the class party, opening valentines, and eating the cupcakes with chocolate frosting before Vinnie grabbed them all.

His mom really lucked out on their birthdays. She hated to cook, so — since he was born near Valentine's Day, and Lacy was born on Halloween — Mom didn't have to send home-baked goodies to school at all. Instead, she let her kids piggy-back class parties.

It was a little embarrassing, but at least their birthday celebrations were bigger and better than anyone else's. Lacy got to wear a costume on her big day, and he got cards from the whole class on his.

Joey glanced at Xia. She'd been watching him all day. Her frequent stare tumbled mixed emotions through his heart. On one hand, he was pleased she'd noticed him, but on the other, her constant attention was a bit unnerving.

Was she trying to send him a mental message right now? Or was she busy reading his mind?

If it was the latter, then she'd know Friday was his birthday because that's what he'd been thinking about. He turned sideways in his desk and

18

focused on her strange eyes. *When is your birthday?* he asked without words.

Joey tensed, blanking his mind, waiting for her birth date to pop into his head.

*Which one?* flashed across his mind like a blinking billboard.

Joey's fingers tightened around the edge of his chair. Which one? What did *that* mean? How many birthdays did a person have?

Unless, of course, she'd died, and. . . . And what, Joey? Been born again? Or raised from the dead. Like a zombie.

"Mr. Ocean, I'm speaking to you."

Joey tore his gaze away from Xia's, ignoring the chuckles echoing in his ears. "Huh?"

Mr. Bramble pulled off his glasses and sighed heavenward, as if he was sure that today would be a wonderful day to retire from his brilliant teaching career.

"I said," he repeated, "do you think your mother can send dessert to school for Friday's party since it's also your birthday?"

Ha! His mom had been caught. No other teacher had ever noticed that Mom was killing two birds with no stones, so to speak.

"Um, I'll ask her," Joey answered, wondering if he should buy a bag of Keebler cookies, scrape off the elves, and pass them off as homemade.

"Let's see," Mr. Bramble muttered, studying his seating chart. "Who else's parents haven't participated in a class party this year?" His pencil stopped, and he glanced at Xia.

Joey's heart stalled. Please don't pick on her again, he thought, trying to send a mind message to the teacher. Mr. Bramble had called on Xia twice this morning, and both times had been a disaster.

The first was during a review of states and capitals. No one could name the capital city of Colorado. Or Wyoming. Or Texas.

Mr. Bramble's next question was intended as a joke: "How many states *are* there?"

Everyone laughed.

Then he called on Xia.

The class grew as quiet as a graveyard. No one had heard Xia speak yet, and they all seemed curious.

Mr. Bramble's answer was Xia's usual blank stare. Then the whole class began to whisper about how stupid she was for not knowing the answer to such a simple question.

But Joey knew that Xia knew. For whatever reason, she chose not to talk. He glared at Suzanne and Mashika, who were pointing at Xia and whisper-laughing about her. He wanted to jump to his feet and scream "Leave her alone!"

But he didn't. Then he felt guilty. Think how *she* felt, knowing everyone in the room believed she was stupid. Could she sense it all at once? he wondered. Or did she read their minds one by one?

The second time Mr. Bramble called on Xia was after he read today's quote from the board. "Who is Oliver Wendell Holmes?" he'd asked. Again, he called on Xia. And again, he got a blank stare.

The funny thing about it was that no one in the room knew the correct answer — *except* Xia. Joey knew because she told him simply by thinking it: *Oliver Wendell Holmes was a famous poet.*

"Oliver Wendell Holmes was a famous poet," Joey had blurted.

A pleased Mr. Bramble beamed, while Vinnie pounded him on the shoulder, making Joey feel miserable for taking credit for Xia's answer. He'd avoided her eyes for the rest of the afternoon.

"Vincent," Mr. Bramble called, breaking his long pause. "How about your mom? Can she send dessert on Friday?"

Mrs. Capaldi was the best parent-cook in the class, and Vinnie knew it. Her Knickerbocker Twirls were even better than the Butterscotch Blintzes Suzanne's father baked. "You bet," he answered, bowing to the cheers.

Joey was relieved that Bram had let Xia off the hook. He gave her a sheepish grin. *I'm sorry I stole your answer*, he said in his mind.

*You didn't steal it. I gave it to you.*

*Touché.* Joey smiled at her silent sarcasm as

21

Mr. Bramble gave a seat work assignment. Everyone began to shuffle papers, sharpen pencils, and whisper.

Everyone except Joey.

Joey's thoughts were still on Xia. It was time someone figured out what was going on with their newest classmate. Since he was the only one who knew for sure that something *was* going on, it was all up to him.

And he knew exactly what to do.

After school, he would follow Xia home. Like the creature who protected the girl in *Night of the Gentle Stalker*.

With that settled, Joey glanced at the clock, checking to see if there was enough time for him to visit the restroom before the final bell.

He copied the seat work assignment into his notebook, then headed toward the door.

Before he could get there, Xia lumbered toward him, her hair continually shifting in the surrounding breeze. As she shuffled by, she slipped something into his hand.

It was the hall pass for the boys' restroom.

# 5.
# Over the River and Through the Woods

J oey waited in the hall by Lacy's classroom. Where was she? If his sister didn't come out soon, Xia would get away before he could hurry outside to see which direction she went.

"Here Rover, here Rover!"

Joey spun around. "Stop that." He glanced at the kids pouring out of classroom doors, and hoped none of them knew what Lacy meant. "Where were you?"

"In the restroom, putting on my Jazzertogs."

"Your what?"

"My exercise clothes." She held up her school clothes to show him she'd changed. "I have to hurry when the bell rings or I'm late to Mom's class."

Joey was so used to seeing his sister in tights and leotards, it didn't faze him that she was standing in the school hall wearing purple tights with a white leotard, splashed with purple kittens and pink balls of yarn.

"I'm in a hurry," she snapped, resting one hand on her bony hip to show him her attitude. "What do you want?"

"When you get to class, tell Mom I . . . uh . . . had some *business* to take care of after school, so I'm not going right home." His mom always called from the Jazzercise Center to make sure he was safe in the house.

"Take care of *business?*" Lacy repeated, yanking up her tights.

Joey read the button she'd pinned onto her leotard: EXERCISE FOR THINNER THIGHS. He wondered if Lacy's skinny bird legs were a good endorsement or not.

"So, what if Mom wants to know what kind of *business* you're taking care of?"

"Look, I gotta go." Joey backed down the hall, not wanting to waste another minute. "Just tell Mom what I said, okay?"

Racing outside, he stopped by the bike rack, not sure which direction to try first. He wasn't too worried about losing Xia. She walked so slowly, surely he could catch up with her.

Groups of kids fanned out from the front and sides of the school building. Xia, who would be easy to find in any crowd, was not among them. Had her mother picked her up while he was waiting for Lacy?

Joey wondered what Mrs. Dedd looked like. He pictured an older version of Xia, so tall, her head stuck out the sunroof of her car as it jerked and swerved slowly down the street. The image made him chuckle, then feel guilty at his irreverence.

On a whim, Joey circled the entire school. He hadn't bothered to look behind the building. The school bordered a thick forest which banked against the bottom of a rocky bluff. There were no houses that way.

But when he got to the rear playground, there she was, walking in that funny stiff way of hers. A row of tall pines edged the soccer field. Xia was heading straight toward them. Where was she going?

Joey waited until she disappeared into the trees. Then he jogged at a slow pace across the soccer field, giving her a chance to get ahead without suspecting that she was being followed.

As he ran, he made up excuses, just in case she caught him. "I left my soccer ball out here," he could say. Or, "Vinnie kicked my ball into the trees this morning, so I came to look for it."

Good. Those were good excuses.

Joey's shoes pounded dully on the half-mushy, half-frozen mud and grass. He zipped his jacket against the frigid air. Icy snowflakes fell from a threatening sky and stabbed his cheeks.

When he got to the border of pines, he hesitated. It was dark in there. Bushes and trees grew thick. Following Xia would not be easy.

But if *she'd* gone in there, well then, so could

he. He suddenly felt competitive, like he did with Vinnie. Whenever they challenged each other, they gave the secret sign they'd made up in the third grade: A flick of the left thumb under the chin. Maybe he should let Xia in on their sign since she was his friend now, too. Sort of.

Joey gingerly moved a wet evergreen bough to one side. A narrow, muddy path wound its way out of sight. He didn't know there was a path through these woods. Of course he'd never looked before. A fresh shoe print in the oozy mud convinced him this was the way Xia had gone.

Joey straightened and took a deep breath. Glancing behind for a last look at familiar surroundings, he gave himself the secret sign, hoping it might make him feel braver than he felt right now. Then he plunged into the dark forest. Why did the sky have to be so dreary today? It made the woods darker than they should be on a late, wintry afternoon.

He tried to be quiet, dodging naked branches that might crack, and hopping over leaves that might crunch, although they looked pretty soggy today. In a matter of minutes, he drew near enough to Xia to tail her without being noticed.

Her bright hair was easy to follow in the drab surroundings. And her awkward movements were hard to camouflage in a forest where bird wings flapped in smooth rhythms, and wind moved pine boughs with sweeping grace.

As Joey followed the curve of the path, the sound of rushing water met his ears, growing louder as he hiked. Around a bend, the path dead-ended into a rock-filled river. Along the banks, the water was frozen white, but in the middle, it flowed fast and deep, drowning other noises in the near distance.

Joey's heart sagged. The idea of swimming an icy river in February was not high on his list of fun things to do. Should he give up and head back the way he'd come?

Then he caught sight of Xia trudging up a hill on the other side of the river. She didn't appear to be wet at all. How did she get across the river and back on the path so fast?

Joey hiked along the water's edge, hopping from rock to rock, slipping twice. Around another bend, the river narrowed. A fat oak tree had fallen from one bank to the other, creating a natural bridge.

Joey sighed. If it wasn't for Xia, he'd give up. Lacy was the daredevil in the Ocean family, not him. If she were here, she'd race across the log in two steps. And if she fell into the river — so much the better. She'd just laugh and swim the rest of the way.

Joey was more apt to collect fallen saplings, rope them together to make a raft, then sail across. But today, time wouldn't allow it. He'd have to take the daredevil route.

Trying not to look at the rushing water, he balanced on the decayed log, holding his arms out straight on each side. The trunk was coated with a thin layer of ice, but the faster he moved, the less he seemed to slip. Near the far bank, a neat line of stepping stones led him from the log to dry ground — and the path.

A sense of pride rushed over Joey as he hustled up the steep bank. He felt pleased at his unexpected bravery; Lacy would've been impressed. She might even have called him by his real name for once.

Hurrying to catch up with Xia, Joey's excitement returned, along with renewed urgency for his task.

When he finally caught sight of her, she was approaching the foot of the bluff. Now what? Did she live here in a cave? With bats and black cats and spider webs?

*"No, Fido,"* Lacy's whiny voice echoed in his head. *"Witches live in caves with bats and black cats and spider webs. Zombies don't. You've got your monsters mixed up."*

Joey groaned at Lacy's words even though his mind had made them up. She was right, of course.

Xia disappeared. Joey edged his way around the sheer rock wall, tripping over low bushes and slipping on wet gravel. His heart began to thump. Was it from the hike? Or was it from fear that the rock wall he was leaning against would suddenly swing loose under his hands, and swirl him inside to a hidden cave?

A cave full of zombies.

"Stop it, Ocean," he whispered to himself. "*Zombie* is Lacy's word, not yours. Xia is just a regular girl." He snagged his jacket on a twig and stopped to pull it free. "Well, maybe not *regular*. Irregular. An irregular girl."

Still, his mind refused to erase the image of himself standing alone in a dark cave with a zillion zombies doing their slow-walk toward him, arms outstretched, eyes staring, mouths gaping.

And all of them hungry. Hungry for living flesh.

*His* living flesh.

# 6.
# Stairway
# to Terror

If Joey hadn't tripped, he might never have noticed the narrow stone stairway angling up the side of the bluff. Xia must have climbed it, but even if she hadn't, his curiosity made him creep up the slippery stairs anyway, staying low, letting the underbrush hide him.

After a hundred steep steps, Joey stopped counting. Pain burnt his thighs with each move. He was sure everyone in the northern hemisphere could hear his heavy breathing. Good thing he wasn't a full-time spy.

Just when his legs couldn't take another step, the stairs ended at a plateau on top of the bluff. Joey hunched on the ground behind the fat trunk of a mulberry tree to catch his breath. Looming in the distance at the edge of the cliff perched a house — a mansion, really, dark and ominous.

Although the wind wasn't blowing, trees around the house whipped as though a blizzard raged. Bare branches waved like skeleton arms, pointing out Joey's hiding place to anyone who might be watching. Broken shutters banged against the peeling paint on the siding. Dead leaves swirled across the walk leading to a rickety veranda.

The scene reminded him of the mansion in *House of Neverending Nightmares*.

"Only this isn't a movie, Ocean," he whispered. "This is real life."

Xia stepped through the gate and turned to shut it. For one long moment, she gazed in Joey's direction. Had she seen him peeking from behind the tree?

As he watched, she crossed the yard, hair blowing as if an invisible fan whirred in front of her. She trudged up the steps to the veranda, then disappeared through the double front doors of the mansion.

Joey sat on the lumpy roots of the mulberry and rubbed his cramped legs, still sore from the climb. "Okay," he said to calm himself. "The girl has merely walked home from school like I do every day. She's probably sitting at the kitchen table right now, having a snack. Her mom is getting ready for Jazzercise, and — "

*G-r-r-r-o-o-o-w-w-w-l!*

Joey's mouth stayed open mid-word while he waited for his frozen blood to melt. "And," he finished in a shaky voice, "her pet monster has just devoured her."

He belly-crawled to the edge of the cliff, prepared to go down the steps head first if a monster burst from the house and roared toward him with fire shooting from all seven eyes. That scene had been in *Monster's Revenge, the Sequel.* He'd never forget it.

Then he thought about Xia's eyes. And her hair. Her tallness. And her ability to read his mind. She was special. He *had* to know more about her. Hadn't she picked *him* to receive her thoughts? That meant she thought he was special, too. Didn't it?

*"Or, it means you're the only one in class with no brain, so there's plenty of room inside your head for Xia's thoughts."*

That was Vinnie's voice. In his mind, of course. At least that's what Vinnie would say if he were here.

"Well, I'm in charge of my thoughts now," Joey snapped, pretending his friend was leaning against the mulberry, arms folded, challenging him to pursue his quest. "I can't leave here until I figure out who Xia Dedd really is, why she lives in such a creepy place, and why she doesn't talk. Out loud."

Joey rose to his feet and tiptoed to the clump of firs near the house. He stayed low, alternating his attention between the house and the gap in the bushes which marked the beginning of the rock stairway. Losing track of his escape route wouldn't be a smart thing to do.

He darted from tree to tree until he was so close to the back gate, he could reach out and touch it. So close, the mysterious gale tousled his hair and ruffled his clothes. Although it was a cold wind, it was not as frigid as the late afternoon air.

A sudden rush of panic made him drop to his knees, feeling safer in the cloak of surrounding bushes. Someone was watching him. He felt naked, exposed. It reminded him of the chase scene in *Feast of the Obese Ogre*.

Peering through the trees, Joey scanned the area, his eyes stopping at every odd-shaped tree trunk, rock, or bush. No one seemed to be there.

*Joey*, a voice called. Not out loud. The name simply exploded inside his mind.

*Joey, over here.*

It was her — Xia. She wanted him to move away from the house, deeper into the forest.

Was it a trick? Was she waiting with others to . . . to what? Turn him into a zombie, too?

*Joey, hurry. I don't have much time.*

The tremble of terror in her voice convinced him she was sincere. And alone, he hoped.

He moved quickly, staying in the shadows, ducking behind a boulder as another ferocious growl split the air. Each was different. The first roar sounded like an angry snarl, the next, a grumble, then a snort, then a howl. All were ear-splitting. And each startled him as much as the first one had.

*Over here.*

Finally, he spotted her. In a grove of lush junipers. Joey hurried to join her, relieved the junipers blocked them from view of the high windows on the third floor — in case anyone was watching.

"How did you know I was following you?" he blurted, feeling miffed at himself for being discovered.

She motioned him to lower his voice. *You didn't follow me. I led you here.*

"You mean — ?"

She touched his lips with one finger to make him stop talking. Fear shadowed her face in the dim light. *Please listen,* she said inside his mind. Only he didn't hear her voice the way he did Vinnie's and Lacy's. It was almost as though her thoughts merged with his own.

*Okay.* He answered back without speaking. *What's going on? Who are you? Why the secrecy? What can I — ?*

She held up a hand. *Stop. I can't transmit my thoughts while you're mind-talking.*

He stifled the questions he wanted to ask, shaking his head to blank them from his mind.

*You've got to help me. My father, too. We . . .*

The growling split the air like a lightning strike. Xia tensed, then shook her head at him in her slow, ponderous way. *There's no time to explain it all now. Please help me.*

Joey nodded. *Yes! Of course I'll help. Tell me what to do.*

*Find the antidote. Then bring it to me.*

*G-r-r-r-r-o-o-o-w-w-w-w-l!*

Xia cringed and backed away. *I have to go in now.*

*Wait!*

She turned, slow-walking deeper into the dark trees.

*But . . .* Joey started after her.

*No.* Xia stopped, twirling toward him in slow motion. Her icy mint eyes grew wide. *You're in danger here.* Panic whitened her face as she stared toward the house. *Go home now. Before it's too late. And find me the antidote.*

*What* kind *of antidote?*

Xia disappeared beyond the junipers, yet her final message burst into Joey's mind like the pop of a firecracker: *The antidote for zombie poison.*

# 7.
# The Clock
# Is Ticking

*Leave the city of your comfort and go
into the wilderness of your intuition.*
— ALAN ALDA

"Mmmm." Joey reread Mr. Bramble's quote for the day. He didn't quite understand what this one meant. He'd have to give it some thought.

Returning his attention to the task in front of him, he guided the blunt tip of his scissors along the pencil line curving across a piece of red construction paper.

The smell of glue and crayons flavored Mr. Bramble's room while the class created valentine decorations for Friday's party.

The fancy heart Joey trimmed with pink paper lace wasn't intended for the bulletin board. He was making a special card for Xia. His hand shook as he thought of her, and the terrified look on her face in the forest yesterday.

He glanced at her empty desk. Where was she today? Did she stay home because she was sick? Or had she been caught sneaking out of her house to meet him?

Was she being punished? What kind of punishment took place in a haunted-looking mansion — home to a mysterious growling monster?

Joey yawned. He'd been up half the night, trying to figure out what an antidote was. Well, he *knew* what an antidote was — something that worked against the effect of poison.

But an antidote for zombie poison? By the time he'd collapsed into bed, he knew more than he ever wanted to know about zombies.

After dinner, his mother had driven him to the library. Joey checked out every book he could find on the topic. Mom, who assumed he was writing a report for school, admired his thorough research. He didn't feel up to explaining the whole weird situation to her.

Back home, poring over the books, he found a lot of surprises. What he thought a zombie was, and what a zombie *really* was, were two different things. He thought they were dead people, brought back to a sluggish life by magic to be kept as slaves.

The truth is that zombies were real, live people

who'd unknowingly been given a cryptic powder. There was no magic. The unique concoction slowed their reflexes so they were at the mercy of their masters.

Still, Joey had questions for which he couldn't find answers. How could something so bizarre happen today? Here in his own town? To someone his age?

And why had Xia come to school? Her master could have kept her in the mansion on top of the cliff, and no one would've known she and her father were there. Had they been kidnapped? Was The Thing That Growls her master?

His last question was the most intriguing: How could Xia possess the power of mind-talking? He hadn't run across *that* in any of the books on zombies.

"Ocean, what's *wrong* with you these days?" Vinnie leaned his elbows on Joey's desk.

"Huh?"

"I *said*, can I borrow your glue?"

"Um, sure. Take it."

Vinnie grabbed the bottle and slid into his seat. "I can't wait till after school," he whispered, glancing at Mr. Bramble. It was okay to talk during art, but not too loudly. "The movie's gonna be great."

"What movie?"

Vinnie whacked his palm to his forehead, then pretended to speak into a walkie-talkie. "Earth to

Ocean. Earth to Ocean. Did you forget Corillo's party this afternoon? His mom's taking us to see that new movie, *Vampires at Camp Tenkiller*.

"Oh." Joey groaned. Yes, he'd forgotten Jimmy Corillo's birthday party at the theater. He'd forgotten to ask his mom if he could go, too, *and* he'd forgotten everything else in the entire universe except a zillion facts about zombies.

"You're coming, aren't you?" Vinnie had glued two of his fingers together. He stuck them straight up so they'd be out of the way as he worked. It looked as if he was holding an invisible cigarette.

"Remember the cool preview?" Vinnie continued. "The vampire sneaks into camp and gets the first guy in the neck?" He dropped the valentine he was gluing and slapped one palm against the right side of his neck, as if hiding bloody vampire marks. "Then the vampire gets somebody else while the guy attacks his best friend." He slapped the other hand on the left side of his neck, then bared what Joey assumed were vampire fangs. Either that, or Vinnie'd had a sudden urge to show Joey his upper molars.

"Then the whole camp turns into vampires." Vinnie's eyes got bigger as his voice got louder. "Their parents come to take them home, and it's like — " He stretched his arms forward and rocked back and forth in his desk, giving Joey a blank stare.

"Vincent Capaldi." Mr. Bramble's voice boomed across the room.

Vinnie dropped his arms.

Joey sighed. "That's not what *vampires* do. That's what *zombies* do. You've got your monsters mixed up."

Vinnie pointed his glued fingers at Joey. "So what makes *you* such an expert on zombies?"

"I'm getting a crash course."

"What?"

"Nothing." Joey had to get out of this. If he went to the movie — as intriguing as it sounded — he'd be wasting precious time. Every minute that ticked by might be putting Xia in greater danger. There wasn't a second to lose. "Look," he said, "I can't go."

"Why not? Is your mommy making you go to Junior Jazzercise?" Vinnie flapped his arms in wiggly waves to one side, then the other, while flipping an invisible pony tail. His sarcasm was exceeded only by his entertaining imitation of Joey's mother.

"Vincent, please quiet down," came Mr. Bramble's voice again as those around snickered.

"That's not Jazzercise," Joey whispered. "That's the hula." He tried to act offended at his friend's teasing, but he really wasn't. Vinnie had a right to give him a hard time. They *always* went to the movies together.

Vinnie's teasing about Jazzercise made Joey remember the hundred-and-something rock steps he had to climb to get to Xia. "Hey, Capaldi, you guessed right." He shrugged his shoulders. "After school, I plan to get some exercise."

The look Vinnie was giving him could win the award for Most Disgusting Look of the Year. If there were such an award.

To avoid further questions, Joey stuck his head into his book bag, scrounging for markers to write a valentine verse to Xia.

The idea of making up a poem for her was a lot easier than actually doing it. He scribbled the usual sentiments: Be mine. Me + you = 4 ever friends. My ♥ beats for you. U R 2 good 2 B 4 me. True love.

Holy jets! Should he use the word *love*? What would she think?

He ripped up the page and started over with something original:

Won't you be my valentine?
I ask this of you, Xia.

Joey's pencil paused in mid-air. What word rhymed with Xia? Mia. Dia. Lia. Korea. Well, yeah, *that* rhymed, but how could he work it into a valentine poem? See ya in Korea?

Dumb, Ocean, he thought. Hey wait. *See ya* works. He added the last two lines:

Let me know your answer soon.
I'm waiting for you — see ya!

Stupid. That's really stupid. So, what kind of valentine do you send to a zombie, Ocean? A zombie valentine? With a verse like:

Roses are dead
Violets are wilted.
Why do you walk
so stiff and so stilted?

Joey's career as a poet was short-lived. He scrunched the second sheet and shoved it into his book bag. He couldn't throw it away in the classroom. Some trash he didn't trust to the garbage can because it might fall into the wrong hands.

Glancing at the clock, his heart sped up. It was time to try it. He didn't know whether or not it would work, but he had to give it his best shot.

In order for Xia to meet him after school, he had to get a message to her. And the only way he could get a message to her was mentally. Would it work this far away?

He squinted his eyes closed and concentrated. *Meet me again in the juniper grove. Meet me again in the juniper grove.*

Still repeating the words, he opened his eyes and studied the paper heart. Then he wrote

## TO XIA

in his best cursive. He'd work on the poem later. Right now it was more important to keep chanting his message.

He had something urgent to tell Xia about zombie poison and its antidote. Something she obviously didn't know.

# 8.
# Undoing the Spell

"Tell Mom I'm taking homework to someone who was absent today." Joey's words tumbled over each other in his rush to get them out so he could leave for the mansion on the bluff.

It wasn't really a fib. He'd tell Xia their homework assignment — if she asked. But they had much more important things to discuss today than the imports and exports of Toronto.

"Who was absent?" Lacy asked, dodging kids in the crowded hall.

Why did she have to be so nosy? "The new girl. What's it to you?"

Lacy's eyes doubled in size. "You mean *her*? The zom — ?"

Joey clapped a hand over Lacy's mouth. "Hush up. Just tell Mom I'll be late."

He stepped into the noisy flow of students before Lacy could argue. Racing outside, he dashed across the soccer field, hoping no one was watching. Then he dived into the darkness of the trees, much less afraid of the unfamiliar forest than he was the day before.

Half-running, half-walking, Joey hurried along the narrow, twisting path. Soon he came to the river whose icy turbulence had unnerved him. But that was yesterday. Today, he hustled across the log bridge like a pro.

By the time he reached the foot of the cliff, he knew he didn't have to climb the torturous rock steps after all. Xia was hiding nearby. He could sense her presence. Or had she *told* him not to climb the steps? Her words blended so smoothly with his thoughts now, he wasn't quite sure *how* he knew she was near.

Joey followed Xia's mental directions. They easily led him to a sandy clearing beyond the base of the stairway. She was perched on a flat boulder. He joined her, wondering if mental small talk was the socially accepted way of opening a conversation without words.

*Well? Did you get it?* she asked.

Her question burst into his mind before he had a chance to sit down. So much for small talk. *No,* he answered.

Xia's shoulders drooped. She started to get up.

*Wait. You don't need an antidote.*

*Oh yeah? Then what do I need?*

Her apprehension ballooned inside his mind until he shared her dismay. *I'll tell you. But first, you tell me a few things. Like what's this all about?*

She raised her eyes toward the cliff high above them, as if afraid someone might be peering over the top, searching for her. *To make a long story short*, she began, *my father and I are being held captive by Dr. Samedi.*

*Dr. Samedi?* Joey echoed.

Xia sighed, as if she knew there was no way Joey would let her get away this time without some answers. *The doctor's research was at a standstill until he could try his experiments on human subjects. Of course, that's illegal, so he's doing it secretly.*

*My father used to be Dr. Samedi's lab assistant at a research center on the West coast, but he never agreed to take part in any experiments. We were tricked into coming here.*

Joey was afraid to ask the big question, but he had to. *Did the doctor turn you into zombies?*

Xia nodded. *All I know about zombie poison and its antidote is what Dr. Samedi told me. He tried to brainwash us, too, by wiring us to a machine and giving us some kind of potion. It worked on my father, I guess, but I fought against the messages from the machine. I sang songs to myself while the machine was supposed to be blanking my memory. It not only worked, but it gave me the power to mind-talk.*

46

Joey stared at her pale face, digesting the incredible story she was telling him. Coming from anyone else, he wouldn't have believed it for a second. But he certainly couldn't deny the evidence of her ability to mind-talk. Not when he'd personally experienced it.

Still, there were lots of unanswered questions. *Why does the doctor allow you to go to school?* he asked.

Xia laughed, but no sound came out. *Some lady in a car with government license plates came snooping around the mansion, and saw me home in the middle of the day. She must have reported Dr. Samedi to the superintendent of schools because a letter came, informing the doctor that he had to enroll me in school immediately, or I'd be placed in a foster home.*

Xia paused to shift her position on the boulder. *He thinks he has me programmed to go to class and come straight home. The poison keeps me from speaking, so he doesn't have to worry about my talking to anyone.*

*But of course he doesn't know about the mind-talking,* she added, glancing at Joey in slow motion. *The doctor figured the teachers would become frustrated with my silence after a few days, label me a slow learner, then recommend a private tutor. That way, the doctor can keep me at the mansion and pretend to be my teacher, home-schooling me.*

47

She was quiet for a few moments. *But if you can't find the antidote that counteracts zombie poison, then I guess. . . .* Her thoughts dissolved into unintelligible mental mumbling.

*Listen,* Joey began, not wanting her to give up. *The antidote keeps the poison from affecting you, but there's an easier way. The master keeps his slaves in a zombie state by giving them poison every day. He has to. One dose doesn't last long. It has to be taken every twenty-four hours.*

*In our food?*

*No. In your shoes. The poison is absorbed through your skin.*

Xia's look of disbelief made him reach for her shoe and yank at the lace. *Look, I did all this research like you asked me to. Now, you've got to believe me.*

Xia helped him with the lace, then pulled off her shoe. They examined it. Nothing. Joey turned her foot upside down. Nothing again. After all the research he'd done, had the doctor outwitted him?

Xia raised one eyebrow. As her thoughts jumbled together again, he tried to translate the message. The exact words didn't come through, but her feelings did. Her feelings of great disappointment.

She stepped into her shoe and began to tie the lace.

*Wait.* Joey pulled her hand away. *Take off your sock.*

*Jo-ey. It's freezing out here and you want me to take off my sock?*

*Do it.*

Xia kicked aside her shoe, and yanked down the sock, turning it inside out as she pulled it off. Something that looked like talcum powder coated the inside. She brushed a few flecks off the bottom of her foot, then stared at Joey.

*Zombie poison* lit up his mind like a movie marquee as they thought it simultaneously.

The powder had an unmistakable odor, very similar to a wild weed that bloomed in the schoolyard during summer.

Xia grinned at him, crinkling freckles around her eyes. It was the first time he'd ever seen her smile. *Bingo*, she said, her hair fluttering about her shoulders like bird wings. *You've cracked the mystery*. She started to put her sock back on.

Joey grabbed it, holding it carefully by the top so none of the powder touched his skin. *Leave it off. And take off the other one.*

She obeyed, wadding both socks into a ball and shoving them into her jacket pocket.

Joey was still confused. *I wonder how the doctor manages to sprinkle the powder into your socks without you knowing it?*

Xia paused, thinking. *He must do it on Saturdays after the dry cleaning service delivers our weekly laundry — and before I put my clean clothes away.*

49

*Makes sense*, Joey thought.

She tied her shoes and jumped to her feet. *So all I have to do is stop wearing socks, then I'll gradually wake up and be normal again, right?*

*Right.* Joey hated to tell her the rest. *But if the doctor figures it out — which he will if you suddenly stop wearing socks — there are other ways he can get the poison to work on you. All it has to do is touch your skin.*

Their minds came to the same conclusion at the same instant: *We've got to destroy his entire supply of zombie poison.*

Xia sighed. *But how?*

Joey stood, brushing dry leaves off his jeans. *Do you know where he keeps the powder?*

*In his lab, I suppose.*

*Can you get inside the lab to dump it?*

Xia's cold mint eyes burned into his. *Only if someone distracts the doctor long enough.*

*Like your father?*

*No,* her mind answered. *Like you.*

# 9.
# It Was a Dark and Stormy Afternoon

Things at home were not going well. Lacy was suspicious about Joey's after-school messages to Mom, and his mother had left him a note this morning saying they needed "to have a little talk."

He hoped today was his last trip to the mansion because he'd be of no further use to Xia if he was grounded for the rest of his life.

Plus, Vinnie thought Joey had gone mental on him when he showed up at the Capaldi house at dinner time, and begged Vinnie to smuggle out three pairs of socks from his dad's dresser drawer.

Joey promised to explain later, since he'd left Xia waiting on the boulder in the forest until he returned with socks that would fit her dad. Socks free of zombie poison.

This morning, the hands on the clock in Mr. Bramble's room were snails, creeping around each hour. Joey tried to hurry them ahead by mind-talking to them. Of course, it didn't work. Yet he could do nothing more to help Xia until school was out.

She wasn't in class today. He'd forgotten to ask her about yesterday's absence, but assumed Dr. Samedi needed her at home. Joey hoped the doctor wasn't trying another strange experiment on her.

Xia had borrowed Joey's socks to wear home last night, so Dr. Samedi wouldn't get suspicious. She would wear them again today, giving herself a whole day off zombie poison to start returning to normal. At least they both hoped the poison wore off that quickly.

Xia's plan was to sneak into her dad's room and replace his socks with Mr. Capaldi's. She'd warned Joey that it might be risky. She and her father had been separated when they arrived at the mansion several months ago. Xia stayed in the east wing of the house and her father stayed in the west wing. She wasn't even sure which room was his.

Of course she couldn't count on her father's help. If he'd been brainwashed, there was no way he could communicate with her.

Finally, *finally*, the dismissal bell rang. Joey was out the door in three seconds, with Vinnie in tow this time. He and Xia had decided an extra person might come in handy — which meant Joey had a lot of explaining to do to his friend. And the look Vinnie was giving him as they jogged across the soccer field told Joey his friend wasn't going to be easy to convince.

"Let me get this straight," Vinnie huffed, his breath puffing out in tiny clouds. "The new girl. The one with the X name. She's in some kind of trouble."

"Danger."

"She's in some kind of danger," Vinnie repeated. "So we're going to her house to help her hide something from the owner so she and her father can get away."

"More or less." Vinnie's version lost a lot in translation.

"Why don't you just call 911?"

"You want me to call the police and tell them a family of zombies is being held against their will on top of the bluff?" Joey gave Vinnie his own version of the famous Disgusted Capaldi Grimace. "First, they'd say I was insane and lock me up, then they'd hunt down Xia and her father as the bad guys instead of the doctor. Xia thinks Dr. Samedi has some kind of logical cover for his operation — in case anyone decides to investigate."

Joey could tell by Vinnie's face that he wasn't too crazy about traipsing through the snowy forest on such a dark and stormy afternoon. When they got to the river, Vinnie balked.

Joey led him along the river's edge to the fallen

log, then crossed easily, showing off a little by pretending to slip. When he reached the other side, Vinnie wasn't behind him. "Come on, Capaldi, it's easy." He flashed his friend the secret sign.

Vinnie, face as pale as the falling snowflakes, slunk across the log on all fours like an overfed dog, growling to himself the entire way. Joey didn't care, as long as Vinnie made it to the other side.

At the foot of the bluff, they began the climb up the rock steps. Behind him, Vinnie's breathing grew louder and heavier. Joey knew if he didn't complain, Vinnie wouldn't either. It was an unwritten rule of competition between them. If one could do it, the other couldn't wimp out.

At the top, they rolled onto their backs, panting for air. It was then, upside down, that Vinnie noticed the mansion. "Holy jets!" he exclaimed, flipping onto his stomach. "What is *that*?"

"Xia's house."

"Why is the wind blowing over there but not here?"

"Probably has to do with one of Dr. Samedi's experiments."

*G-r-r-r-o-o-o-w-w-w-l-l-l!*

Vinnie leaped to his feet and lunged for the stairs. Joey grabbed the cuff of his jeans, making Vinnie fall hard onto his stomach.

"What was that?" he gasped, hugging the ground.

"I don't know." Joey rolled behind the fat mulberry so he couldn't be seen from the house.

"You don't *know*?" Vinnie hissed. "We could be eaten alive by a monster who growls like a hungry shark, and you don't *know* what it is?"

Rising to his knees, Joey peered around the tree. "Hungry sharks don't growl. Hungry grizzlies do."

"Grizzlies?" Vinnie raised his head, whipping it from side to side as he scanned the forest.

"Or hungry tigers."

"Stop it." He pushed to his knees. "So how come Xia doesn't know what's making all the noise?"

Joey shrugged. "She's never run into it, but she said it can sense when anyone or anything is on top of the bluff."

"Any*thing*?"

"Like an animal. Movement in the area sets it off. Our job is to confuse it, make it think there are tons of people — or animals — on the bluff so it keeps growling."

"Why?"

"To confuse Dr. Samedi enough to make him leave the house to investigate. That will give Xia a chance to sneak into the lab and find the zombie poison."

"The what?"

"That's what makes her the way she is."

"Zombie poison?" As Vinnie jumped to his feet, Joey yanked him behind the mulberry.

Vinnie peeked around the gnarled tree trunk. "Man, this is spookier than *Phantom in My Footsteps*."

"That was a movie. This is real life."

"This is *your* real life. I'm gettin' out of here."

Joey was tempted to let Vinnie go. He didn't want to waste any more time arguing while Xia waited for them to do their part. Yet, support from his friend might make the task easier. "Please stay, Capaldi. I need your help."

He gave Vinnie the secret sign again. "Friends till the end, remember?"

"Yeah, friend. And this is the end." Vinnie dropped to his knees to crawl to the steps.

*G-r-r-r-o-o-o-w-w-w-l-l-l!*

Cringing, he scrambled back to the tree for cover. "I hate it when that happens."

"Look!" Joey pointed toward the mansion.

A zombie, taller than any human could possibly be, lumbered across the yard and opened the back gate. It was a man, so thin his clothes hung limp upon his frame. Long, flowing hair blew about his shoulders. A full beard stretched almost to his belt.

"Is he coming after us?" Vinnie's voice was breathy from fear. He covered his eyes with both hands.

"I hope not." Joey wanted to cover his eyes, too, but he was fascinated by the sight. Was it Xia's father? Was he coming to help them? Or was he in league with the evil doctor?

Joey remembered the brainwashing machine, and decided to stay hidden. He didn't want to take any chances.

Vinnie peeked through his fingers. "If you call a zombie by name, it breaks the spell," he whispered.

"No, it doesn't. It breaks the spell on were-wolves. You've got your monsters mixed up again."

"You have to drive a stake through its heart. It's the only way."

"No, no, no. That's how you kill Dracula."

The instant the words were out of his mouth, Joey's heart flip-flopped. That voice wasn't Vinnie's. It was — "Lacy! What are *you* doing here?"

She flashed her toothless grin. "Hi, Spot. I wanted to see where you went every day after school, so I followed you."

"*Spot?*" Vinnie murmured.

Lacy plopped to the ground. "Boy, those steps are murder."

"La-cy!" Joey hissed an octave higher. "Why'd you do this?" He wanted to shake her by the scrawny shoulders for ruining his plan. "Now I've got *you* to worry about, and. . . ."

His angry words jumbled together, making it

impossible to get any of them out. Jumping to his feet, he paced as best he could without stepping out into the open. "Mom's gonna kill me." He tried to yell quietly — which was hard. "You're a *witch* for doing this, Lacy. An ugly old witch — with warts!"

Her bottom lip quivered, but Joey didn't care. All those years of Lacy rubbing in Milford's saga pumped more anger through him than seeing her show up here on the bluff — and calling him *Spot* in front of Vinnie. "On the Halloween night you were born," he snarled, "the most hated witch in the world died, and came back as *you!*" He kicked the trunk of the mulberry to punctuate his statement.

Lacy's face turned red and wrinkly. "I am *not* a witch," she whimpered. "Don't call me that." She held her breath to keep from crying because it made her angrier when Joey called her a crybaby.

And he would.

"Lacy witch. Lacy witch. Lacy witch."

"Oh, man," Vinnie groaned, crawling toward the steps.

Joey grabbed his friend's jacket, turning his frustration on Vinnie. "Look," he barked through clenched teeth. "You're here and you're going to *stay* here. To help Xia. She's counting on us."

He glanced at the zombie man, still checking the area around the house in slow motion, searching for whatever was triggering the *Thing* to growl. "And you," he snapped at Lacy. "You're going to help, too."

"Me?"

Joey expected her to act frightened, shrink away, turn and race down the stairs to safety. But instead, her daring fearlessness rose to the surface.

"Really?" she added, as if Joey had just told her she'd won a complete wardrobe of Jazzertogs.

"Yeah, really." His anger became diluted with admiration at how quickly she rose to a challenge. He wished *he* could do that. "I can't take you home now, so you've got to stay here and help."

Lacy grinned, rubbing her hands together as if it was a game they were about to play. Joey only wished it were. He tried not to think what his mother would do to him if Lacy got hurt on his account.

"Vinnie, you take the back of the house," he ordered. "I'll go around to the far side. Lacy, you stay here, and — and listen to me, and do what I say. If anything scares you or comes after you, make a beeline down those stairs, understand?"

She jumped to her feet and gave him her attitude stance. "I'll help only if you stop calling me Lacy witch."

He put his face in hers. "I'll stop calling you a witch, if you quit calling me Spot. And Rover. And Fido."

She bent to one side, bouncing from the waist a few times, then lunged forward as if warming up to consider his offer.

"Lacy witch. Lacy wi — "

"Okay, okay." She aimed a scissor-kick at his chest, forcing him back against the tree trunk. "I'll quit."

"Would you two *stop*?" Vinnie yelped. "The walking dead is on his way to rip off our living flesh, and you're having a family feud."

Vinnie's words snapped Joey back to his purpose for being there. He pulled the others into a huddle. "Okay, here's the plan. Make lots of noise and movements. But stay out of sight. Do all the distracting you can — without being caught. Got it?"

Vinnie stopped him. "You gave your sister permission to get the heck out of here if she wants to. What about me?"

"You can run faster than a zombie can walk."

"What if Dr. Samedi comes after me?"

"He's a grownup. You can outrun a grownup."

Vinnie didn't look convinced.

Joey straightened, peeking around the tree once more. "Is everybody ready?" He tried to inject confidence and enthusiasm into his voice — at least more than he was feeling right now.

"We're ready," his partners echoed.

Without looking back, Joey dashed into the

shadows, keeping one eye on the house, and one eye on the zombie man. He only wished he could trade in his bumbling partners for one who was less sarcastic, and for one who wasn't dressed in neon flowered tights.

# 10.
# The Thing
# That Growls

Joey sprinted between two outcroppings of rock, moving fast, hoping he wouldn't be seen by the zombie man, the Thing That Growls, or by anyone else who might be watching from one of the high windows.

As he moved, the monster growled and snarled, howled and groaned, screamed and roared. The Thing must be sensing the movements of all three of them. Good. Joey hoped Dr. Samedi was so distracted that he was on his way out of the lab right this very minute.

Feeling like the spy in *Secret Agent of Horror*, Joey worked his way to the far side of the mansion, then moved from tree to tree, tossing rocks toward the cliff's edge to confuse whatever was monitoring movement on the estate grounds.

The closer he got to the house, the more furiously the wind raged. Watching from a distance, the gusts hadn't seemed this strong. But as he moved nearer, Joey was forced to lean into the gale, holding one hand to block dirt and twigs from blowing into his eyes.

What was the purpose of Dr. Samedi's home hurricane? To discourage Girl Scouts selling cookies? Wouldn't a twenty-foot concrete wall do the same thing? This guy really valued his privacy.

Joey squinted into the fake storm. Where was Xia? He'd mentally pictured the path he'd taken, just in case she was trying to figure out where he was.

In his thoughts, he wished her luck, too, and hoped there was some way she could let him know if her plan worked. He tried not to think what might happen if it backfired. How could he make sure she was safe? What if he never saw her again?

A loud tapping drew his attention toward the tall, arched windows along the side of the mansion. Someone waved to him in frantic motions. It was Xia, tugging at the window, forcing it open. She motioned for him to come inside.

Joey's enthusiasm fizzled like a popped balloon. Dashing bravely about the grounds of the mansion was one thing. Going inside the house was another. That would be . . . well, *dangerous*.

*Hurry!* Xia's pale face seemed paler in the dim light. Her command inside his head seemed faint, too. Maybe the turbulence around the grounds affected her ability to mind-talk.

Joey dashed toward the house, hopped over the railing onto the veranda, then stopped. Or rather, his fear stopped him. He'd agreed to help Xia by coming here and creating a distraction. And he'd done that — fulfilling his part of the bargain. Now it was time to find Lacy and get home before Mom . . .

*Jo-ey!*

He was close enough to see the desperate, pleading look in her eyes. Her hair danced wildly about her shoulders. Even her freckles seemed to hiphop around her face as the wind whipped.

Still, Joey did not *want* to go inside. Ocean, she needs you, his mind told him.

Every cell in his body screamed for him to bolt in the opposite direction. Then Mr. Bramble's voice echoed inside his head: *"Leave the city of your comfort and go into the wilderness of your intuition."*

Ah, now he knew exactly what it meant.

*Please, Joey. Now!* Xia leaned out the window, urging him closer.

Joey shivered — more from her plea than from the wind cutting through his jacket as if it wasn't there. A broken branch flew toward the veranda as if someone had flung it at him. Joey ducked, then took the final three steps to the window. "You want me to come inside?" he hollered above the tornado roar. Wonderfully intuitive of you, Ocean, he added to himself.

In answer, Xia lunged over the ledge and grabbed his wrists, yanking him into the house head first. He somersaulted forward, then sprang to his feet in case someone else was in the room, waiting to pounce on him.

Someone like Dr. Samedi or the Thing That Growls.

But he and Xia were alone. In a turn-of-the-century parlor.

Joey moved cautiously around the ornately decorated room, blinking to adjust to the dim light. He rubbed his hands together to warm them. It was good to be out of the artificial storm.

Xia slammed the window shut to block the howling wind. Now it was quiet. Deathly quiet.

He studied his surroundings. A brocaded settee with a white doily on each armrest perched on a flowered rug. Crystal vases in various colors decorated tiger-claw tables. Flames flickered in oil lamps on the fireplace mantel. Everything in the parlor looked the same as it must have a hundred years ago — including the dust.

Joey started to sneeze.

Xia shook her head and waved both hands at him.

He held his breath until the urge to sneeze passed.

"Come on." She led him across the room.

"Hey, you talked!" he exclaimed in a loud whisper.

She tried not to smile, but he could tell she was pleased. "The effect of the powder is wearing off.

I can move faster, too, see?" She demonstrated by shuffling double-time across the worn rug.

Joey didn't want to disappoint her, but she still walked like a seasick penguin. He wondered how long it would be until she could take human-size steps.

Xia led him down a shadowy hallway. Gray cobwebs clung to the walls like loose wallpaper.

*Where is the doctor?* Joey asked without words.

She didn't answer.

Her ability to mind-talk must be fading, too. He repeated the question verbally.

"The doctor went outside to see what's going on," Xia answered. *"Finally.* It's our only chance to get into his lab."

"Then why are we being so quiet?"

"That growling thing. I don't know where it is."

She disappeared down an unlit stairwell to the cellar.

Great, he told himself. That growling thing. She doesn't know where it is. And here we are, heading down a dark stairway to heaven knows what. I love surprises.

Joey tried not to react to the narrow staircase, the creaking steps, and the musty, dusty smells mingling with strange odors rising from the lab. He felt as though he was on his way to a dungeon deep inside a haunted castle.

His ears began to tingle as they thawed in the warmth of the stuffy house. He wondered why the turbulent storm could not be heard inside. More of Dr. Samedi's magic?

At the bottom of the steps, the stairwell curved to the left. A huge metal door blocked their way.

"This is why I need your help," Xia whispered, leaning her shoulder against the door.

Joey shoved as hard as he could. The door barely moved. No way could she have opened it by herself. They pushed until it cracked enough for them to squeeze through.

Xia gasped as she stepped into the lab.

"Holy jets," Joey whispered, joining her. The brightly lit room looked futuristic — a complete turnaround from the rest of the dusty mansion. Everything was white or chrome, or blinking and flashing. Shelves were piled high with computer storage tapes and CDs. Boxes of supplies were stacked randomly around the polished white floor. Pots boiled on a twenty-first century stove with no burners.

One wall was a massive control panel, with more computer equipment than the Starship Enterprise — or so it seemed to Joey.

A messy work island filled the center of the room. Several experiments-in-progress cluttered the top of the counter, along with boxes of books with such titles as *Is it Magic? Or is it Science?* and *Things People Think Don't Exist.*

Joey opened the second book. Chapter one was: The True History of Time Travel Machines and

How You Can Build One. Before he could read further, Xia gave another gasp.

"There it is," she exclaimed, running to an odd-looking machine standing in a row of other strange contraptions.

Reluctantly, Joey closed the book and followed her. "What are they? Torture machines? Brain-washing machines?"

From the look on Xia's face, he knew the latter was the correct guess. Grabbing a handful of wires, she yanked them free. Then, using both hands, she tore at the rest of the cables as if she wanted to ensure that the machine could never be used again.

Joey watched for a few moments. Should he help her destroy the machine that tried to destroy her mind? "Come on," he finally said, putting a hand on her shoulder. "This is not what we came here to do."

Xia nodded, flinging a knot of broken wires across the floor.

She chose one side of the room while Joey took the other. Slowly they scanned shelves packed with jars, boxes, and flasks. Reading labels, they searched for containers filled with zombie poison.

One high cabinet was locked. They decided to search for the key as they worked their way around the room.

Joey's curiosity made him want to stop and examine bottles marked *Gravity Neutralizer*

(Directions: take only until your feet leave the ground or you'll rise too high).

Or *Language Unscrambler* (for instant speaking, reading, or understanding any language).

There were flasks marked *Tallness*, *Shortness*, *Thinness*, *Wrinkle Eliminator*, *Freckle Fader*, and even *Bald Reversal.*

"This guy's a genuine wizard," Joey muttered, wondering if a sprinkle of *Shortness* would make him the same height as Vinnie and the other guys in the sixth grade.

"Joey, look!" Xia's excited voice drew him across the room to the control panel. A slick-looking CD player blinked "in use" in red digital letters. Xia pointed to the program name flashing on a monitor. *Ferocious Animal Imitator.* "Is this what I think it is?"

Joey studied the control panel. It listed speaker locations around the estate. A mixing board controlled the volume at each area. He chose "Rock Steps," then shoved the volume lever to "loud."

Xia pushed the *test* button. *G-r-r-o-o-w-w-l-l-l!*

Joey jumped, laughing in embarrassed relief. So there *was* no monster guarding the mansion. Just another one of Dr. Samedi's quirky inventions.

Joey thought about Lacy. He'd told her to stay by the rock steps. Well, he hadn't *meant* to scare her, but if he had, he hoped she was scared so badly, she was dashing home this very minute.

"And look!" Xia pointed to another panel. The LED display said *Whirlawind* in flashing blue letters. "I'll bet this is how he creates a storm around the house." She clicked off the switch, then squinted through the high, narrow cellar windows. Instantly the gusts of wind quieted, the trees stood still, and the leaves in the yard stopped swirling.

The breeze surrounding Xia stopped, too. "Oh, good," she mumbled, finger-combing her tangled hair. "It'll be much easier to sleep now."

Nothing else on the control panel looked important, so they went back to their search for the powder.

"Ah, ha!" Xia exclaimed after a few moments. Her voice was muffled because her head was stuck inside a cabinet under the sink.

"Did you find it?" Joey raced across the room, kneeling to see what had captured her attention.

"I found something else." She pointed at two bottles sitting side by side. One was marked *Mind Enhancer*, and the other *Mind Eliminator*.

"The doctor has poor eyesight." She picked up the *Mind Enhancer* and read the label. "Yep, this explains why I'm able to mind-talk instead of being brainwashed." Xia sighed. "Lucky for me. Unlucky for my dad."

A noise upstairs made them jump. As they

scrambled behind an L-shaped counter, Joey tripped over a cage of gray laboratory rats. The door sprang open, and the rats, making tiny chirping noises, scurried in all directions.

Xia didn't scream or run or do any of the girl-things Joey expected her to do at the sight of a dozen rats running loose. It made him like her all the more.

Instead, she yanked him below the counter out of sight from whoever was clunking down the steps.

"We shouldn't have turned off the *Whirlawind*," Joey whispered. "Now Dr. Samedi knows someone is in his lab."

Joey's heart thumped in fear of the doctor, even though a little sympathy had crept inside after seeing all the man's inventions. The doctor had spent a lifetime making incredible discoveries that had to be tested in secret. How bad could a person who invented *Freckle Fader* be?

Bad enough to turn innocent people into zombies, he reminded himself.

A buzzing sound made Joey peer between two stacks of computer tape piled on top of the counter. The heavy door swung open. "There's a hidden button to move the door," he whispered as he ducked out of sight.

Voices captured Joey's attention: "Why are you such a big meanie?" someone was asking.

The voice! He recognized it instantly. Lacy!

Dread filled Joey's chest. The evil Dr. Samedi had kidnapped his little sister!

Joey leaned against the counter and smacked his hand against his head. "No, no, n-o-o-o," he groaned as quietly as he could. "All I need now is a zombie sister."

# 11.
# We're Off to
# See the Wizard

"**I**'m not a big meanie, my dear girl," the doctor was saying. His accent sounded too much like Dracula's to put Joey at ease. "I am a humble scientist who wants to be left alone to my research. I refuse to be bothered by federal restrictions, applications for grant money, or ridiculous state regulations."

"Why do you keep a horrible monster locked up in your house?"

"Come," he said. "Let me show you the horrible monster." Footsteps echoed across the room, then the fake monster growls played tag with Lacy's giggles as she pushed the button over and over. Howls and growls, near and far, reverberated around the estate.

"Great," Joey whispered. "She'll probably ask if she can take it home with her."

"Can I take it home with me?"

"Oh, I don't think so," the doctor said. "It has

become my friend and protector. I call him Tigger. Heh, heh."

How quaint, Joey thought with a shudder. Wonder what he calls his torture machine? Pooh Bear?

Rising to his knees, he peeked over the counter top, curious to see what the doctor looked like. He seemed as ancient as the house, with unkempt white hair sticking out from under a bowler hat, and a ragged beard in need of a trim.

He wore a dirty lab coat that looked as if it'd been through more years of experiments than it had trips through a washing machine. His shoulders were stooped from long hours bent over the computer keyboard or his high-tech lasers, Joey assumed.

Lacy was wandering around the room, studying pictures, touching things she probably shouldn't be touching, and poking at the strange machines. "Show me how you make a zombie," she blurted.

Joey heard the doctor's sharp intake of breath. "How does one so young know about such things?" he asked, placing a hand over his heart.

"Well, my brother Joey is a friend of Xia's, and he said you gave her zombie poison to make her walk like this."

Lacy had moved behind a pillar. Joey couldn't see her, but he knew she was doing her straight-arm, slow-dance zombie impersonation.

The doctor's laugh sounded forced. "It's just an

experiment, my dear. I'm almost finished with her."

Xia and Joey exchanged glances.

*Finished?* Xia mouthed. *Then what?*

"Then what?" asked Lacy.

Dr. Samedi was quiet for a moment, thinking. "Then, well, there are other experiments I'd like to try on human subjects. And now, I seem to have quite an abundance of — shall I say — guinea pigs?"

The doctor's words shivered a chill through Joey. An abundance? Two wasn't an abundance. Four was. He must be counting Lacy and me. And Vinnie? Joey wondered if his friend was still playing slow motion hide-and-seek with the zombie man.

His legs started to ache from their cramped position. He had no intention of staying here and letting the doctor use him as a guinea pig. Maybe he should make a break for the metal door. Could he get there before the doctor reacted?

As Joey turned to tell Xia his plan, the door clanged shut. Dr. Samedi must have installed buttons around the room to open and close the door at will.

"Terrific," Joey mumbled, grimacing at Xia. Now they were trapped.

Meanwhile, the doctor was explaining guinea pigs to Lacy, who seemed convinced that pet pigs were hidden in cabinets around the lab.

"What have you done with my brother?" Lacy demanded. "Have you kidnapped him and turned him into a pig already?"

"Heh, heh, heh."

There was something about the doctor's laugh that Joey hated as much as being duped by fake growling from a fake monster.

"You can't trick my brother," Lacy said. "He's the tallest boy in the sixth grade."

Was his sister actually bragging about him? Joey was touched.

"Xia is his girlfriend and I think they're in *love*." Lacy emphasized the word *love* as if that mattered to the doctor.

Joey could feel a blush burning its way up his neck. A real growling monster couldn't force him to turn and look at Xia, although the sound of her quiet snickering was a blow to his ego.

"Don't worry about your brother," said the doctor. "Let's worry about *you* for a minute." He paused. "Now, what should I do with such an opinionated young lady?"

"Show me the zombie poison," Lacy said, as if the doctor meant he was planning to entertain her.

He cleared his throat. "Oh, no, miss. It's far too precious to — "

"I want to see it!" Lacy screamed, bursting into tears.

"All ri-ight," Joey whispered, urging her on.

He knew his sister was only pretending to be upset. It took a lot to make her cry. He should know — he'd tested her limits many, many times.

"Now, now," the doctor said, acting flustered by the tears. He opened a cupboard and took out a box of tissues.

Lacy howled louder, stamping her foot with each new wave of sobs.

"Well, I suppose it wouldn't hurt if you took a *peek* at the zombie powder," he said with a great sigh. "But you must be very, very careful." He moved to the locked cabinet on the far wall, pulling a key from his shirt pocket.

"So *that's* what's under lock and key," Xia whispered.

Joey knee-walked to the edge of the counter to see better.

The doctor gingerly lifted a flask from the shelf as though it was filled with Tinker Bell's magic fairy dust. Holding it up to the light, he gazed affectionately at the contents.

Joey hesitated. Should he make a dash for the flask? What would he do with it? The locked door blocked his escape, and the basement windows were too high.

Where had the doctor been standing when the door swung shut? Maybe Xia could locate the button while Joey distracted the doctor, then . . .

"Hey." Xia was right behind him, practically breathing down his neck. "What should we do?"

she whispered. "This is what we've been waiting for."

Dr. Samedi held the flask over Lacy's head, as if he wanted her to look up through the bottom of the glass and not get any closer.

Just as Joey started to answer, Lacy did a Jazzer-bounce and snatched the flask from the doctor's grasp. "Got it!" she shouted.

Dr. Samedi grabbed for her, but she was too quick. "Stop!" he cried. "It's dangerous!"

Since the door was closed, the only place to run was around the work island in the middle of the room. "I'm going to save Xia and Joey!" Lacy screamed. "Where are they?"

Joey dashed from behind the counter and dived for his sister. He missed, sprawling on the floor. "I'm here, Lacy! Give me the flask!"

A startled Lacy Jazzer-hopped over a stack of CDs. "Look, Joey," she yelped. "*I'm* the one who found the zombie poison!"

Dr. Samedi high-jumped over Joey, dodged Xia, who tried to block his path, then climbed over the CDs after Lacy. "Drop it!" he shouted. "No! I didn't mean that. Don't drop it. Give it to me!"

Xia raced after them with Joey close behind. Lacy was small enough to dive under tables and scuttle through to the other side. Unfortunately, that's where the lab rats were hiding. Disturbed, they joined the race, too.

Suddenly, the floor seemed to be moving, but

it was only gray furry bodies and pink noses and tails, along with terrified rat shrieks.

When Lacy saw the rats, she froze, shrieking louder than all of them.

Then she threw both hands over her head, and dropped the flask of zombie poison.

# 12.
# The Showdown

Tiny white granules flowed across the floor like powdered sugar, mixed with broken flecks of glass. Lacy leaped on top of a table, screaming, and doing jazzer knee-lifts to get away from the rats.

The others skidded to a stop to keep from stepping in the powder. All except the rats. They zigzagged right through it, their feet and undersides turning white with zombie poison.

Everyone gasped. There was no way to stop the rats.

"Blast it!" cried Dr. Samedi. "That's all the powder I have." He glared at Lacy, his face as red as the digital numbers on the control panel. "Do you know how long it takes to assemble ingredients for a single dose, young lady? You think it's easy finding live snake hearts, petrified walrus tusks, and bloated sea toads?"

*Gross!* Joey made a sick face at Xia. Good thing

she didn't have to drink the powder, only step in it.

Dr. Samedi fetched a broom. He was so distraught, he seemed to forget that Joey and Xia were in the lab — as if there were anywhere else they could possibly go. Lacy was still frozen on top of the table, keeping both eyes on the wandering rats. The rodents seemed to be moving slower, bumping into things, confused.

All the fear Joey harbored for the doctor dissolved. What he saw now was an eccentric old man whose treasured "magic" formula had just been scattered across the dirty floor. It might have taken his entire lifetime to create it.

Just as Joey started feeling sympathetic, the doctor turned on him. "You!" he shouted. "This is all your fault!" He began to sweep with a vengeance, billowing clouds of powder into the air.

Joey jumped back as the smell of summer weeds filled the lab. He hoped inhaling the odor wouldn't make him walk funny.

"You'll pay for your meddling," the doctor added. "Xia! Bring me the bottle marked *Formula Shrink*." He jabbed the broom handle toward a row of chrome shelves with glass doors.

*Formula Shrink?* Joey and Xia exchanged glances. Was Dr. Samedi planning to try one of his experiments on Joey? Right here and now?

Xia started to speak, then stopped. Turning,

she slow-walked toward the row of bottles sitting on the shelves.

Good, Joey thought. She's pretending to be under the spell of the zombie poison. The doctor hasn't figured it out yet. He's too upset to register the fact that she was dashing about the lab only minutes ago.

Ignoring Dr. Samedi's evil glare, Joey grabbed the waste can near the sink, and carried it to the spill so the doctor could sweep his precious powder into the trash. The sooner the powder was disposed of, the better, as far as Joey was concerned.

Dr. Samedi seemed surprised by Joey's kindness. "Are you thirsty, son?" he asked, feigning kindness in return.

Joey shrugged. He had a feeling that whatever *Formula Shrink* was, the doctor planned to quench Joey's thirst with it.

Xia was taking her time, walking slower than she did when the powder was working on her full force.

"I might as well tell you my plan," the doctor began. "Since none of you are going anywhere." He scooped the rest of the powder into the waste can, then hung the broom on a hook. Its weight caused the wall panel to swivel around, storing the broom in a hidden compartment.

"Someone is bound to come snooping around here as soon as it's evident that a couple of kids have disappeared," Dr. Samedi continued. "And when they do, you'll be right here — only they won't see or hear you."

Pausing, the doctor scrubbed his hands in the sink to remove any powder that might have settled onto his skin. "And the reason they won't see or hear you is because, after a couple swallows of my cherry-flavored treat, you'll be smaller than a rat's tear."

Smaller than a rat's tear? Joey's mind echoed.

Xia was moving too slowly for the doctor's liking. He dried his hands vigorously, then flung the towel onto the counter and rushed across the room, snatching the bottle from her hand.

"We're not thirsty, sir," Joey began, not knowing quite how to address him. "And we don't take food from strangers, so you can't make us dr — "

The doctor had whipped a handkerchief out of a drawer with a pair of tongs, and pressed it against the back of Joey's neck.

The instant it touched him, he froze. His legs felt like tree trunks, shooting roots deep into the house's foundation. He tried to lift his hand to brush off the handkerchief, but his arms seemed glued to his sides. And his mouth stayed open, mid-word.

"What were you saying about not drinking?" Dr. Samedi asked. "Heh, heh, heh."

"*I'm* thirsty," Lacy piped up. She'd been so busy monitoring the movement of the rats, she hadn't been paying attention.

"*Shut up, Lacy,*" Joey tried to say, but the words refused to come out. They sort of rattled around inside his mouth, like coins in an empty can. He wondered if that's how Xia had felt when she tried to talk under the influence of the zombie poison.

"Well, young lady, I won't disappoint you." Dr. Samedi faced Joey. "Watch closely what this shrink drink does to your sister, young man." He swished the liquid in the bottle. It fizzled like cherry pop. "Because you will take the next few swallows. Then your girlfriend will finish it off."

Joey tried to run. He tried to speak. Then, as the panic of the moment flooded over him, he tried to scream.

He could do nothing.

They were doomed.

# 13.
# Zombie Rats

**D**r. Samedi opened a cabinet and took out three paper cups. He poured a tiny amount in the first one, then stopped and squinted at Lacy, as if determining how large a dose to give her. He dribbled in a little more.

Xia glanced frantically from Joey to Lacy.

*Do something!* Joey yelled at her, even though he knew her power to mind-talk was gone.

As if she'd gotten his message, Xia moved in slow-motion toward Lacy, trying to catch her eye, while still pretending to be a zombie.

"Well, young lady," Dr. Samedi said, replacing the lid on the bottle. "Since you're thirsty, how about some cherry soda?"

Lacy was staring at Joey with a puzzled look on her face, as though trying to figure out what was going on. "What's wrong with my brother?" she asked.

The doctor ignored her question. "Here." He thrust the drink at her.

As Lacy reached for the cup, a loud commotion upstairs made everyone jump — everyone except Joey since he was still paralyzed in the same position.

Shouting and barking and the pounding of shoes on the steps tensed his muscles. His eyes moved side to side, urgently searching for the button to release the metal door.

"Drink this!" Dr. Samedi shouted. He forced the cup into Lacy's hand, spilling a few drops on a notebook. Instantly, the notebook shriveled to the size of a postage stamp, shooting off a quick puff of gray smoke.

Dashing to the counter, the doctor fumbled with the paper cups for a few long moments, then brutally shoved them aside. Unscrewing the lid on the bottle, he rushed to his next victim, raising the drink to Joey's already-open mouth.

The buzzer sounded as the metal door swung open. A barking dog lunged into the lab, followed by two police officers, followed by the skinny, long-haired zombie man, followed by a white-faced Vinnie.

At the same moment, Xia lunged between Joey and the doctor, knocking the bottle of *Formula Shrink* against the doctor's chest, then onto a chair. Instantly, the chair disappeared. Or seemed to disappear. The chair became smaller than a rat's tear, instead of the three of them.

Dr. Samedi desperately wiped at the formula

with the sleeve of his lab coat, but it was too late. His coat began to shrink. The seams tore across his shoulders and down his arms, pop-pop-popping like corn kernels as they ripped apart. The coat, in tiny pieces, floated to the floor.

Under the coat, his tie shrank, choking him. Gasping for breath, he yanked it free as the buttons on his shrinking shirt popped off, bouncing and skipping like tiddlywinks across the tile floor. The seams burst, and his shirt slipped from his shoulders, catching at the waist by his belt. The sleeves fluttered to the floor.

Everyone in the room gaped at Dr. Samedi, waiting to see what else was going to happen. Xia snatched the tongs from the counter and yanked the cloth off Joey's neck.

Joey sprang away from the doctor, shaking his arms and legs, grateful his frozen condition wasn't permanent.

Confusion dominated for a few minutes while Xia shouted at the officers to keep the dog from lapping up the red liquid. The doctor, now down to an undershirt that read: LABORATORY ANIMALS NEVER HAVE A NICE DAY, recovered his composure and grabbed another lab coat off a hat rack.

"Hey, Ocean!" Vinnie yelled from the doorway. "I called in the cavalry — just like in *Werewolf Soldiers!*" He thumbed his chin, giving Joey their sign.

Meanwhile, the zombie man and Xia were rushing toward each other.

"Dad!" she cried, hugging him.

So it *was* Xia's father.

Dr. Samedi was staring at Dr. Dedd and Xia in amazement. "You can speak. You can move."

"Thanks to this young man," Xia's father said, pointing at Joey, "we have overcome the zombie poison."

Joey modestly dropped his gaze and stepped around the red puddle on the floor, kneeling to pet the police dog. He didn't want to take credit for everything when it was really Xia's plea to help that motivated him.

The police officer loosened his grip on the dog's leash to allow him to sit while Joey gave his neck a good scratching. "Are you all right, son?" the officer asked.

Joey nodded.

"I'm Officer Jaffurs," he said, "and this is Captain Wardlaw." He nodded at the other officer. She was clicking handcuffs around Dr. Samedi's wrists.

The dog was soon distracted, sampling all the unusual scents. Pulling away from Joey, he sniffgrowled here one second, there two seconds. Pure canine heaven.

"It was a puzzle to me how the poison was being administered," Dr. Dedd continued. "I stopped eating, hoping I'd snap out of it, but Joey here is the one who discovered that the powder was being absorbed through the skin of our feet. My daughter explained it all in a note she left in my shoe after switching my socks." He shook his head. "Absolutely brilliant."

Joey wondered if Dr. Dedd meant that *he* was brilliant for solving the mystery, if Xia was brilliant for getting rid of the powdered socks, *or* if the doctor was brilliant for inventing the zombie poison.

Xia grinned up at her father. "I thought you were brainwashed."

"And I thought you were." He gave her a fatherly pat on the shoulder. "I was pretending, just like you, so the doctor wouldn't realize his failure in the brainwashing attempt."

The canine corps finished inspecting the lab. "No illegal substances here that Bruiser can detect," the officer said to Captain Wardlaw. He led the dog toward the stairs.

Joey wished Bruiser would stay so he could play with him. Bruiser was a cool dog. Why couldn't Milford have been a cool dog instead of a wimpy mutt? Joey would be proud to go through life as Joseph Bruiser Ocean.

A loud sniffle reminded Joey that his sister still teetered on the table top, clutching the cup of *Formula Shrink* in one hand. He hurried across the room and grabbed the cup, setting it in an out-of-the-way spot until he could dump it outside.

Pouring it down the sink might cause the pipes to shrink.

Joey lifted Lacy off the table. He'd have to remember her fear of rodents. It might come in handy some day.

After he set her on the floor, she high-stepped a few times, not quite ready for her feet to touch the ground, even though the rats had hidden themselves again. Joey wished circumstances were different so he could ask Dr. Samedi to try out his *Gravity Neutralizer* on Lacy. Seeing his sister hover above the floor would really be neat.

Dr. Samedi and Dr. Dedd began a heated discussion about formulas and measurements and the correct way to conduct an experiment.

Joey thought it was kind of hard to take a man seriously when his hair was longer than his daughter's. He seemed shorter now, too — not as tall as he had appeared when Joey first saw him. Was super-human height a side effect of zombie poison? Or an optical illusion created by the doctor?

"Excuse me," Captain Wardlaw said, interrupting them. "Dr. Dedd, I really need to read Dr. Samedi his rights and take him to the station."

"I don't plan to press charges," Xia's dad said.

"You don't?" That came from everyone in the room, including the doctor.

"No," he answered. "I've had a chance to observe Dr. Samedi more closely here than I did back home at the research center. I found the hidden button, allowing me to get into the lab, then I studied his inventions while he slept. And look at this." He ran a hand through his long, thick hair. "The top of my head used to be as bald as a newborn baby's," he exclaimed. "Then I borrowed some of Dr. Samedi's *Bald Reversal*, and my hair grew back. And look what it did for my beard. It's a miracle!"

Captain Wardlaw sneaked a bored glance at her watch, but the balding Officer Jaffurs looked very, very interested in Dr. Dedd's new hair.

"I think Dr. Samedi has a lot to offer the world," Xia's father continued. "And he can't do it from behind prison bars."

"Well, that's very noble of you," Captain Wardlaw said. "But the fact remains that this man is guilty of kidnapping, and . . . and attempting to shrink people, so I believe the decision is out of your hands."

Dr. Dedd bowed to the captain's authority.

Dr. Samedi allowed himself to be taken into custody. "I'll make a deal with you," he said to Xia's father. "I'm flattered that you've taken such an interest in my work. If you agree to carry on with my research while I am . . . uh . . . indisposed, I will have the lab and everything in it shipped back to the research center. Deal?"

Dr. Dedd looked as if he'd just won the whole-earth lottery. He winked at Joey and Xia. "Deal," he said. "And, when *I'm* the boss," he added, pointing to a spaced-out rat, slow-creeping 'round and 'round in a dazed circle, "we'll find a way to test our experiments without harming anyone — including innocent rats."

# 14.
# Zombie Valentines

Joey borrowed a red marker from Vinnie to write the finished poem on Xia's valentine. He had to hurry because Mr. Bramble told them Xia was coming back after lunch only long enough to collect her things, share a few minutes of the class party, and say good-bye before she and her father left for the airport.

His heart felt slow and heavy at the thought of her leaving, almost as if it'd had a healthy dose of zombie powder.

He wished Xia didn't have to go, but he was happy she'd soon be back in her own home and her own school. With her own friends.

And boyfriend? his mind added, sprinkling his thoughts with jealousy.

Joey studied his valentine with pride. The glue had dried without glumping, and none of his pencil lines showed. And he was proud of his verse:

*We all will miss you when you leave because we think you're fine. If you get lonely when you're home call 555-2489.*

Joey wanted to say *I* will miss you when you leave, but he wasn't brave enough. Yeah, you're brave, Ocean, he told himself. Didn't you help Xia foil Dr. Samedi's plan? That took a lot of bravery.

Joey pondered over how to sign his name. Yours truly? Sincerely? Your friend? (Boring, Ocean.)

"Here she comes!" cried Vinnie.

Joey shot his friend a suspicious look. Why Vinnie's sudden enthusiasm? Did he like Xia now, too?

She stepped into the classroom amid cheers. Even from Suzanne and Mashika. This morning, the class had gotten to watch news coverage of the "raid" on the Samedi mansion because Mr. Bramble videotaped it last night.

After everyone heard her story, Xia was pronounced class hero for the day, although she asked to share the honor with Joey and Vinnie.

Stopping at the front of the room, Xia took a helping of punch and cookies — Mrs. Ocean's famous almost-homemade Keebler cookies, Joey noticed with pride.

He watched her for a moment, then glanced at Mr. Bramble's daily saying on the chalkboard:

*You must do the thing you think you cannot do.*
—Eleanor Roosevelt

Joey picked up a red pen and scrawled across the bottom of his valentine:

*Love, Joey*

He was no Milford wimp.

He helped Xia clean out her desk. She dumped everything into a box Mr. Bramble had given her. "Thank you for helping," she said to Joey, smiling up at him.

Wait a minute. Joey stared, as if seeing her for the first time. How could he look *down* at her if they were the same height?

Then he noticed her hair. It wasn't as bright as October anymore. It was a muted, deep auburn, more like November. And her eyes. They were still green, but not mint ice cream green. More like pine needle green. They were warm now, too, instead of icy, as she watched him.

He knew without asking that the zombie poison had completely worn off. Xia was just a regular, normal, ordinary girl. Well, maybe not. She was still the first girl who'd made his heart turn upside down.

"This is for you," he said, handing her the valentine.

She read it, ducking her head with a sudden shyness. "There's a mistake on it," she said.

"There is? Where?"

She pointed at her name. "Xia isn't my real name. Dr. Samedi changed it. He says all zombies have names that begin with the letter X."

"Oh." Joey was sorry he'd ruined her valentine. But it was an honest mistake. "What's your *real* name?"

"Jennifer."

"Jennifer?" Joey felt a bit disappointed. He knew a hundred Jennifers. *Xia* was different. Special. To him, she'd always be Xia.

"The doctor renamed my dad Xavier," she added, giggling.

Joey liked her so much better now that she could laugh.

Xia finished her punch, crunching the cup into a ball. "Dr. Samedi also says a person is reborn when he becomes a zombie. That's why I told you I had more than one birthday."

"Ah," Joey said. "At last, the answers are coming. So, what's your real *last* name? The ol' doctor *really* blew it there. He must have used his own brainwashing machine and couldn't think of anything better. *Dedd* — ha! That's got to be the weirdest name in the world." Joey bent over, laughing.

Xia's face was a shade of purply pink. "Dedd *is* my real last name," she answered without a smile. "The doctor didn't change it."

"Oh." Joey wished he could melt through the floor and keep melting until he arrived in another country where saying stupid and embarrassing things was expected and admired.

"Here." She thrust a valentine at him. "I have to go. My dad's waiting outside in a taxi."

Joey read the valentine. It simply said:

Candy and flowers
won't fill the hours
until I hear from you.
Please keep in touch,
I'll miss you so much,
'cause guys like you are few.

She'll miss me! Joey felt unusually warm for a chilly February afternoon. Her poem was mushier than his! "Thanks, Xia, uh, Jennifer."

She shoved a gift at him. "And this is for your birthday. It's a book on zombie lore called *Meet the Dead*. But I didn't write it." She chuckled at her own joke, so Joey laughed with her.

Then she said good-bye to the rest of the class.

And walked out of Joey Ocean's life.

He sighed as he reread the valentine, searching

to see how she signed her name. It wasn't there. Joey's ego felt as if he'd swallowed a double dose of *Formula Shrink*. She'd forgotten to sign his valentine.

Rushing to the window, he watched Xia climb into the taxi.

*Turn it over.*

Joey's temperature zoomed. He turned the valentine over. On the back was a heart. Inside the heart, it said:

Love, Jennifer

Joey gasped. Did he *think* "turn it over?" Or did Xia . . . ? No, she couldn't have. She didn't have special powers anymore. Did she? Or was he getting his monsters mixed up again. . . .

Tucking the valentine safely into his back pocket, Joey returned to his desk and opened the zombie lore book to the Table of Contents. He wanted to see if there was a chapter on how to make zombie valentines.

If not, well then, maybe he could write one.

# About the Author

DIAN CURTIS REGAN is not a zombie — unless awakened too early in the morning. She is the author of many books for young readers, including *The Kissing Contest* and *Liver Cookies*. Ms. Regan grew up in Colorado Springs, and graduated from the University of Colorado in Boulder (Go Buffs). She presently lives in Edmond, Oklahoma.

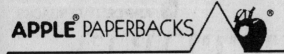

# APPLE® PAPERBACKS

## Pick an Apple and Polish Off Some Great Reading!

### BEST-SELLING APPLE TITLES

| | | |
|---|---|---|
| ❏ MT43944-8 | **Afternoon of the Elves** Janet Taylor Lisle | **$2.75** |
| ❏ MT43109-9 | **Boys Are Yucko** Anna Grossnickle Hines | **$2.75** |
| ❏ MT43473-X | **The Broccoli Tapes** Jan Slepian | **$2.95** |
| ❏ MT42709-1 | **Christina's Ghost** Betty Ren Wright | **$2.75** |
| ❏ MT43461-6 | **The Dollhouse Murders** Betty Ren Wright | **$2.75** |
| ❏ MT43444-6 | **Ghosts Beneath Our Feet** Betty Ren Wright | **$2.75** |
| ❏ MT44351-8 | **Help! I'm a Prisoner in the Library** Eth Clifford | **$2.75** |
| ❏ MT44567-7 | **Leah's Song** Eth Clifford | **$2.75** |
| ❏ MT43618-X | **Me and Katie (The Pest)** Ann M. Martin | **$2.75** |
| ❏ MT41529-8 | **My Sister, The Creep** Candice F. Ransom | **$2.75** |
| ❏ MT42883-7 | **Sixth Grade Can Really Kill You** Barthe DeClements | **$2.75** |
| ❏ MT40409-1 | **Sixth Grade Secrets** Louis Sachar | **$2.75** |
| ❏ MT42882-9 | **Sixth Grade Sleepover** Eve Bunting | **$2.75** |
| ❏ MT41732-0 | **Too Many Murphys** Colleen O'Shaughnessy McKenna | **$2.75** |

**Available wherever you buy books, or use this order form.**

------------------------------------------------

**Scholastic Inc., P.O. Box 7502, 2931 East McCarty Street, Jefferson City, MO 65102**

Please send me the books I have checked above. I am enclosing $_____ (please add $2.00 to cover shipping and handling). Send check or money order — no cash or C.O.D.s please.

Name _____

Address _____

City_____ State/Zip _____

Please allow four to six weeks for delivery. Offer good in the U.S.A. only. Sorry, mail orders are not available to residents of Canada. Prices subject to change.

APP591